P9-DWS-691

CALGARY PUBLIC LIBRARY

AUG 2017

To my parents

KH

For my niece Charlotte

JW

little bee books

An imprint of Bonnier Publishing USA
251 Park Avenue South, New York, New York 10010
Illustrations copyright © 2016 by Jo Williamson
Text copyright © 2016 by The Templar Company Limited
This little bee books edition, 2017.
All rights reserved, including the right of
reproduction in whole or in part in any form.
LITTLE BEE BOOKS is a trademark of Bonnier Publishing USA,
and associated colophon is a trademark of Bonnier Publishing USA.
Manufactured in China 0081216
First Edition
2 4 6 8 10 9 7 5 3 1
ISBN 978-1-4998-0437-9
littlebeebooks.com
bonnierpublishingusa.com

Petunia Paris's Parrot

by Katie Haworth illustrated by Jo Williamson

little bee books

Every year before Petunia Paris's birthday,
Petunia's parents asked her what present she would like.

Her fifth birthday was no different.

Petunia Paris thought. And thought. And thought.

She already had a swimming pool.
(That was last year's present.)

She already had a city of toys.
(That was from the year before.)

She also had a thousand dresses, her own personal library, and a bicycle with its own chauffeur.

Petunia couldn't think of a single thing she wanted. And so she said the first thing that popped into her head.

"I would like a parrot please, most perfectest Mommy and Daddy."

So Petunia's parents organized the usual birthday party . . .

. . . which was splendid, of course . . .

. . . and her present was given to her with a flourish.

It was a beautiful scarlet macaw all the way from Peru.

Petunia was pleased with her parrot.

She had heard that parrots were great conversationalists, so as soon as the last guests had gone home, Petunia stood and waited for it to speak.

But all it said was *Squarrk!*

It was not a pretty sound.

It was NOT a promising start.

But Petunia Paris was an extremely determined young lady,
and so she decided to persevere.
She tried plying him with exotic food . . .

. . . presenting pertinent topics of conversation . . .

. . . playing him the piano . . .

. . . and planning preposterous new outfits for him.

TA-DA!
Squarrk!

But none of Petunia's ploys prevailed.
And the only thing her parrot said was:

After months of trying her best to make her parrot talk,
persistent Petunia finally lost her patience:

WHAT DO YOU WANT FROM ME?

"Excuse me," said the butler, "might I make a suggestion? Suppose you try asking him nicely, Miss Paris?"

So Petunia politely enquired, "Please, Mr. Parrot, I was wondering if you would be so kind as to tell me why you won't speak to me? Is there something wrong?"

And it was then that the parrot spoke . . .

"I DO NOT WANT
a perfectly presented pile of prawns.

I DO NOT WANT
a pleasantly played piano solo.

I DO NOT WANT
to ponder parrot philosophy.

I DO NOT WANT
to wear a pink parrot poncho.

I DO NOT WANT ANY of it, Petunia Paris!"

Petunia Paris was rather perturbed.

But she still had the presence of mind to ask him one more question:

And Petunia Paris's parrot said very softly:

Every year before Petunia Paris's birthday, Petunia's parents asked her what present she would like. Her sixth birthday was no different.

This time Petunia Paris did not need to think at all.

"Can we go to Peru please, most perfectest Mommy and Daddy?"

It was a very long journey to Peru,
but Petunia Paris's parrot did not stop
talking the whole way there.

And Petunia Paris's sixth birthday party was very different from any she'd had before.

Squarrk!